PEOPLEIZE

Chapter 1

Decolonizing Money for Global Equality

Utilizing Currency for Equity, Not Colonialism

By Einar Ourlove

PEOPLEIZE

This is a work of fiction. All of the characters, organizations, and events portrayed in this novel are either products of the author's imagination and are being used fictitiously in this novel.

Copyright ©

Our books may be purchased in bulk for promotional, educational, or business use. Please contact your local bookseller or us directly at info@einarourlove.com

www.einarourlove.com
www.peopleize.world

Originally published 2024

Dedication

In solemn remembrance and heartfelt tribute, this book is dedicated to the over 10,000 Palestinian Children massacred by merciless onslaught of the Israeli military of the Palestinian people in the Genocide of Gaza during just the first 100 days. Their innocent lives, marked by unwarranted suffering and unimaginable loss, serve as a poignant reminder of the profound human cost of conflict.

May the collective cry's of these young innocent Children echo through the pages of this book, resonating across the globe, and inspiring a universal call for a stop to all wars, violence and all people's of earth to live in peace. In dedicating these words to the precious lives murdered, we aspire to ignite a transformative conversation about the imperative need to abandon violence as a means of resolving our differences.

May the memories of the Palestinian children be a catalyst for change, motivating people worldwide to seek paths to dialogue, diplomacy, and comprehensive peace with each other. In their honor, let us unite in our commitment to building a world where conflicts are resolved through courts of law, cooperation, and a shared vision of peaceful coexistence. May their legacy be a guiding light, urging us all to work tirelessly towards a future where every child can grow and thrive in a world free from the shadows of violence and war.

Contents

Chapter i

Decolonizing from the Shackles of Financial Colonialism

Financial colonialism, deeply entrenched in history, finds its origins in the era of European colonial expansion. Colonial powers not only sought to exploit the abundant natural resources and labor of colonized territories but also imposed financial systems designed to serve their imperial interests. This historical backdrop is essential for comprehending the enduring legacy of financial colonialism and its modern-day manifestations. In contemporary contexts, financial colonialism persists through various mechanisms, shaping the economic landscapes of nations formerly subject to colonization. Defined as the exploitation and domination of economic systems by external powers, financial colonialism continues to exert influence through mechanisms such as debt dependency, currency manipulation, and unequal trade relationships. At the heart of this exploitation lies the use of **paper money** as a tool of post-colonial control, symbolizing economic subjugation and dependency for many nations. Its impact extends beyond transactions, shaping entire economic structures and perpetuating systems of inequality and injustice. In this chapter, we delve into the historical context of financial colonialism, explore its contemporary manifestations, and analyze the profound implications of paper money as a tool of post-colonial control.

Historical Context of Financial Colonialism:

The historical context of financial colonialism reveals a systematic imposition of colonial financial systems by European powers on colonized territories, exemplifying a stark manifestation of economic exploitation. Colonial rulers leveraged financial structures as a means to extract wealth from colonies, consolidating their dominance and accruing riches at the expense of indigenous populations. One poignant example of this exploitation is the British Empire's imposition of the Sterling Area system across its colonies, which tied their currencies to the British pound, effectively ensuring economic subservience to the empire. In addition, the Dutch East India Company's control over the currency systems in its colonies in Southeast Asia exemplifies how financial structures were used to solidify colonial control and siphon resources back to the imperial center.

The introduction of paper money emerged as a pivotal tool in this process of economic subjugation, facilitating the seamless flow of resources from colonies to colonial powers. Traditional currencies indigenous to colonized territories were supplanted by colonial currencies, often backed by the economic and military might of the ruling empire. For instance, during the Scramble for Africa in the late 19th century, European colonial powers introduced their own currencies in African colonies, displacing existing monetary systems and exerting control over local economies. This transition not only facilitated economic exploitation but also systematically eroded local autonomy and sovereignty, further entrenching colonial dominance.

Furthermore, the imposition of colonial financial systems had far-reaching implications for indigenous economies and societies. The forced integration of colonized territories into global economic networks through colonial currencies disrupted traditional economic practices and trading systems. For example, in India, the British colonial administration imposed the British pound as the official currency, displacing indigenous monetary systems and undermining local economic autonomy. This imposition led to widespread economic dislocation and social upheaval, exacerbating poverty and inequality among indigenous populations. Similarly, in the Caribbean, colonial powers imposed plantation economies and enforced a system of debt bondage, where indigenous populations were forced to use colonial currencies to repay debts owed to colonial authorities, perpetuating cycles of economic dependency and exploitation.

The historical context of financial colonialism underscores the systemic nature of economic exploitation by colonial powers and highlights the enduring legacy of colonial financial systems in shaping post-colonial economic landscapes. The introduction of paper money as a tool of economic control played a central role in facilitating this exploitation, amplifying the economic disparities and injustices inflicted upon colonized peoples.

In Africa, particularly in regions formerly under French colonial rule, the legacy of financial colonialism persists through a unique system known as the "Franc Zone" or "Franc CFA" (Communauté Financière Africaine). Established during the colonial era and maintained after independence, the Franc Zone comprises fourteen African countries that use the CFA franc as their currency. These countries include Benin, Burkina Faso, Guinea-Bissau, Ivory Coast, Mali, Niger, Senegal, Togo, Cameroon, Central African Republic, Chad, Republic of Congo, Equatorial Guinea, and Gabon.

The Franc CFA system traces its origins to the French colonial administration's imposition of the CFA franc as the official currency in its African colonies. Initially pegged to the French franc, and later to the euro, the CFA franc is issued and guaranteed by the French Treasury. This arrangement effectively ties the monetary policy of Franc Zone countries to that of France, limiting their ability to pursue independent monetary policies tailored to their economic needs.

Critics argue that the Franc CFA system perpetuates a form of financial colonialism, whereby African countries are deprived of monetary sovereignty and forced to prioritize the interests of the French Treasury over their own economic development. The pegging of the CFA franc to the euro, coupled with stringent currency convertibility requirements, restricts the ability of Franc Zone countries to devalue their currencies to boost exports or stimulate economic growth. Additionally, the requirement for Franc Zone countries to deposit a portion of their foreign exchange reserves with the French Treasury further undermines their economic autonomy and hampers their ability to respond to external shocks.

Moreover, the Franc CFA system has been criticized for perpetuating unequal trade relationships between African countries and France, whereby former colonial powers benefit from preferential access to African markets and resources. This arrangement has been likened to a form of "neocolonialism," whereby African countries remain economically dependent on their former colonial masters.

Despite these criticisms, proponents of the Franc CFA system argue that it provides stability and credibility to the currencies of Franc Zone countries, thereby fostering investor confidence and promoting economic integration within the region. However, calls for reforming or dismantling the Franc CFA system have grown louder in recent years, with some African leaders advocating for greater monetary autonomy and the establishment of a common African currency free from external control.

Modern Manifestations of Financial Colonialism:

In contemporary times, financial colonialism persists through various channels, perpetuating economic inequality and dependency in post-colonial nations. Central to this phenomenon is the manipulation of paper money, which serves as a tool of control by external powers. Central banks, often influenced by global financial institutions, wield significant power over monetary policy, shaping economic conditions in post-colonial nations. For instance, in many African countries, the monetary policy decisions of central banks are heavily influenced by former colonial powers or international financial institutions, such as the International Monetary Fund (IMF) or the World Bank. This influence often manifests in the form of conditional loans and policy prescriptions imposed by these institutions as a condition for financial assistance or debt relief. As a result, central banks in post-colonial nations may find themselves compelled to adopt monetary policies dictated by external actors, even if these policies are not aligned with the country's long-term economic interests.

These external pressures often prioritize objectives such as price stability, fiscal austerity, and currency stability, which may conflict with the broader developmental goals of post-colonial nations. For example, under IMF and World Bank programs, African countries may be required to implement tight monetary policies aimed at curbing inflation and stabilizing exchange rates. While these policies may benefit foreign investors and creditors by enhancing macroeconomic stability, they can also constrain domestic investment, hinder job creation, and exacerbate poverty and inequality.

Furthermore, the influence of former colonial powers on monetary policy decisions may perpetuate historical patterns of economic exploitation and dependency. Post-colonial nations may continue to rely on former colonial powers for technical assistance, training, and expertise in central banking and monetary policy, reinforcing asymmetrical power dynamics in the global financial system. This reliance can undermine efforts to develop indigenous capacity and promote economic self-sufficiency, perpetuating a cycle of dependency on external actors for economic governance.

Moreover, the dominance of former colonial powers and international financial institutions in shaping monetary policy decisions can undermine the sovereignty of post-colonial nations and limit their ability to pursue independent economic strategies. African central banks may face pressure to prioritize the interests of foreign investors and creditors over the welfare of their own citizens, sacrificing long-term development objectives in favor of short-term financial stability.

In this way, the influence of former colonial powers and international financial institutions on monetary policy decisions in African countries underscores the persistence of financial colonialism in the post-colonial era. Addressing this influence requires efforts to strengthen domestic institutions, enhance policy autonomy, and promote inclusive decision-making processes that prioritize the interests of local communities and promote sustainable development.

Currency manipulation is another prominent feature of modern financial colonialism, contributing to economic disparities and perpetuating dependency in post-colonial nations. External powers may manipulate exchange rates or impose fixed currency regimes that favor their own economic interests, thereby limiting the ability of post-colonial nations to pursue independent monetary policies. This manipulation can result in overvaluation or undervaluation of domestic currencies, adversely affecting trade balances and hindering economic development.For example, the Asian Financial Crisis of the late 1990s vividly exposed the vulnerabilities of countries like Thailand and Indonesia to speculative attacks on their currencies, thereby highlighting the detrimental impact of currency manipulation on post-colonial economies. During this crisis, speculative investors targeted the currencies of these Southeast Asian nations, triggering a rapid and severe depreciation in their exchange rates. This sudden currency devaluation sparked a chain reaction of economic turmoil, leading to sharp declines in asset prices, widespread bankruptcies, and severe economic recessions across the region.

The roots of the Asian Financial Crisis can be traced back to structural weaknesses in the financial systems of these countries, compounded by external factors such as currency manipulation and speculative attacks. In the years preceding the crisis, Thailand and Indonesia had experienced rapid economic growth fueled by large inflows of foreign capital and excessive lending by domestic banks. However, these booms were built on fragile foundations, characterized by weak regulatory oversight, excessive corporate borrowing, and unsustainable asset price inflation.

As the vulnerabilities of their financial systems became apparent, speculative investors seized upon perceived weaknesses in these economies to mount attacks on their currencies. Utilizing sophisticated financial instruments and leveraging their market dominance, these investors engaged in massive short-selling of Thai baht and Indonesian rupiah, triggering a collapse in their exchange rates. The sudden depreciation of their currencies undermined investor confidence, leading to capital flight, banking crises, and sovereign debt defaults.

The consequences of the Asian Financial Crisis were profound and far-reaching, affecting millions of people and exposing the fragility of post-colonial economies in the face of external shocks. In Thailand and Indonesia, the crisis resulted in soaring unemployment, widespread poverty, and social unrest, as businesses collapsed, banks failed, and government revenues plummeted. The crisis also had spill-over effects on neighboring countries in the region, exacerbating economic instability and undermining regional integration efforts.

Moreover, the Asian Financial Crisis laid bare the detrimental impact of currency manipulation and speculative attacks on post-colonial economies, highlighting the urgent need for reforms to strengthen financial regulation, enhance macroeconomic stability, and promote sustainable development. In response to the crisis, affected countries implemented far-reaching economic reforms, including measures to strengthen banking supervision, liberalize capital markets, and diversify their economies. These reforms, while painful in the short term, helped to rebuild confidence, restore stability, and lay the foundations for more resilient and inclusive economic growth in the long term.

Debt dependency is a significant mechanism through which financial colonialism perpetuates economic subjugation in post-colonial nations. Many post-colonial countries, burdened by external debts accumulated during the colonial era or through loans from international financial institutions, find themselves trapped in cycles of debt repayment. These debts often come with stringent conditions imposed by creditors, such as structural adjustment programs or austerity measures, which further exacerbate poverty and inequality. For instance, countries in Latin America and Africa have grappled with the enduring consequences of debt burdens accumulated during the 1980s debt crisis, constraining their ability to invest in critical social services and infrastructure. The 1980s debt crisis was precipitated by a combination of factors, including excessive borrowing by governments, volatile interest rates, and declining commodity prices, exacerbated by economic mismanagement and political instability in many borrowing nations.

During this period, Latin American and African countries borrowed heavily from international financial institutions and commercial banks to finance ambitious development projects and spur economic growth. However, when global economic conditions deteriorated, and interest rates soared, many of these countries found themselves unable to service their mounting debts. As a result, they were forced to turn to international creditors, such as the International Monetary Fund (IMF) and the World Bank, for emergency assistance and debt restructuring.

The terms of the debt restructuring agreements imposed by international creditors were often stringent, requiring countries to implement painful austerity measures, such as deep cuts to public spending, privatization of state-owned enterprises, and deregulation of financial markets. These austerity measures exacerbated social inequality and contributed to widespread poverty, as governments were forced to prioritize debt repayment over investments in essential social services, such as education, healthcare, and infrastructure.

Furthermore, the debt burdens accumulated during the 1980s debt crisis continue to weigh heavily on the economies of Latin American and African countries, diverting scarce resources away from productive investments and hindering long-term development prospects. Debt service payments often consume a significant portion of government budgets, leaving little room for investment in poverty alleviation programs or infrastructure development. Moreover, the high cost of servicing external debt constrains the ability of these countries to access new financing for much-needed investments in areas such as education, healthcare, and renewable energy.

The cycle of debt and austerity perpetuates a vicious cycle of economic underdevelopment and dependency, as countries remain trapped in a cycle of borrowing and debt repayment, without ever fully escaping the burden of their past debts. Addressing the legacy of the 1980s debt crisis requires a comprehensive approach that includes debt relief initiatives, reforms to strengthen domestic revenue mobilization, and policies to promote sustainable and inclusive economic growth. Additionally, efforts to address the root causes of debt accumulation, such as corruption, weak governance, and unsustainable borrowing practices, are essential to prevent future debt crises and promote long-term economic stability and development.

Unequal trade relationships also contribute to the perpetuation of financial colonialism in post-colonial nations, limiting their economic agency and exacerbating dependency on external powers. Post-colonial countries often find themselves locked into exploitative trade agreements that prioritize the interests of former colonial powers or multinational corporations. These agreements may result in the exploitation of natural resources, the stifling of domestic industries, and the perpetuation of economic dependency. For example, the extraction of natural resources such as oil and minerals in many African countries continues to illustrate the enduring legacy of exploitation and economic disparity, where foreign corporations and former colonial powers reap substantial profits at the expense of local communities and sustainable development. Despite possessing vast reserves of valuable natural resources, many African nations remain mired in poverty, inequality, and environmental degradation, as the benefits of resource extraction disproportionately accrue to external actors rather than local populations.

Foreign government and corporations, engage in extractive activities to exploit Africa's abundant natural wealth for commercial gain. These corporations typically operate under agreements that grant them access to mineral-rich lands or offshore oil reserves, often at the expense of indigenous communities who rely on these resources for their livelihoods. In many cases, these agreements are negotiated behind closed doors, with little transparency or consultation with affected communities, leading to widespread land dispossession, environmental degradation, and social conflict.

Furthermore, the extraction of natural resources in Africa is often characterized by exploitative labor practices, environmental degradation, and human rights abuses. Local communities living in proximity to extractive sites frequently bear the brunt of these adverse impacts, experiencing displacement, loss of livelihoods, and exposure to toxic pollutants. Moreover, the revenue generated from resource extraction is often siphoned off by corrupt officials or elites, rather than being reinvested in local development projects or social welfare programs.

Former colonial powers also play a significant role in shaping the dynamics of resource extraction in Africa, leveraging their economic and political influence to secure favorable terms for resource exploitation. Historical legacies of colonialism, including unequal trade relationships and neocolonial interventions, continue to shape the extractive landscape in Africa, perpetuating patterns of economic dependency and exploitation. Western corporations, backed by their governments, often wield considerable power and influence in negotiating contracts and accessing natural resources in African countries, further marginalizing local communities and hindering sustainable development efforts.

The persistence of extractive industries in Africa highlights the urgent need for reforms to ensure that resource extraction benefits local communities and contributes to sustainable development. This requires greater transparency and accountability in the negotiation of extractive contracts, as well as mechanisms to ensure that revenues from resource extraction are reinvested in local development projects, poverty alleviation programs, and environmental conservation initiatives. Moreover, empowering local communities to participate in decision-making processes related to resource extraction is essential to safeguarding their rights, promoting social justice, and fostering inclusive economic development in Africa.

Despite achieving political independence, many post-colonial nations remain ensnared in a cycle of economic subjugation perpetuated by the legacy of financial colonialism. The manipulation of paper money, currency manipulation, debt dependency, and unequal trade relationships continue to limit the economic agency and sovereignty of these nations, hindering their efforts to achieve sustainable development and economic justice. Addressing the modern manifestations of financial colonialism requires concerted efforts to reform global financial systems, promote economic empowerment, and foster genuine partnerships based on mutual respect and equity.

Impact of Paper Money as a Tool of Post-Colonial Control:

Paper money, introduced by colonial powers to replace traditional currencies, has entrenched itself as a symbol of economic subjugation and dependency for many post-colonial nations. Its introduction was often accompanied by policies that favored the interests of colonial powers and external creditors over the economic well-being of local populations, shaping economic structures and perpetuating systems of inequality and injustice.

One significant aspect of paper money's impact is its control by external powers, a dynamic that severely limits the monetary sovereignty of affected nations. Central banks in post-colonial countries often find themselves subject to the monetary policies dictated by former colonial powers or international financial institutions, such as the IMF or World Bank. This lack of autonomy effectively undermines the ability of these nations to pursue independent economic strategies that are tailored to their specific needs and circumstances.

For example, many African countries that were formerly colonized by European powers continue to grapple with the legacy of colonial monetary systems that were designed to serve the interests of the colonial rulers. The Franc Zone, comprising countries that use the CFA franc as their currency, exemplifies this lack of monetary sovereignty. The CFA franc is pegged to the euro and guaranteed by the French Treasury, effectively tying the monetary policy of these countries to that of France. As a result, these countries have limited control over their own monetary policies and are unable to independently address economic challenges such as inflation or currency devaluation.

Similarly, in Latin America, countries that were subjected to neoliberal economic policies imposed by international financial institutions in the 1980s and 1990s continue to struggle with limited monetary sovereignty. These policies, often prescribed as conditions for receiving loans or debt relief, emphasized fiscal austerity, deregulation, and privatization. While these measures were intended to promote economic stability and growth, they often had detrimental effects on local economies, leading to increased inequality, unemployment, and social unrest.

Furthermore, the influence of international financial institutions such as the IMF and World Bank extends beyond policy prescriptions to encompass broader economic governance frameworks. Many post-colonial nations are required to adhere to international monetary standards and reporting requirements set by these institutions, further constraining their ability to implement independent monetary policies. This lack of autonomy not only undermines the sovereignty of these nations but also perpetuates systems of economic dependency and exploitation inherited from the colonial era.

The control of paper money by external powers represents a significant barrier to the monetary sovereignty of post-colonial nations. This lack of autonomy limits the ability of these nations to pursue independent economic strategies and address the unique challenges they face. To overcome this legacy of economic control and exploitation, post-colonial nations must assert their sovereignty and pursue policies that prioritize the well-being and development of their own

The devaluation of local currencies, driven by external influences, further exacerbates economic disparities within post-colonial societies. Devaluation reduces the purchasing power of local currencies, making imported goods more expensive and fueling inflation. This inflation disproportionately affects low-income individuals and vulnerable populations, who are least able to absorb the rising costs of essential goods and services. Moreover, devaluation can undermine confidence in the local currency, leading to capital flight and exacerbating economic instability.

Furthermore, the use of paper money as a means of debt repayment perpetuates cycles of indebtedness and economic exploitation in post-colonial nations. Many of these countries accumulate significant levels of external debt, often incurred during the colonial era or through loans from international financial institutions. The repayment of these debts, denominated in foreign currencies, places a heavy burden on the economies of post-colonial nations, diverting resources away from essential social services and infrastructure development. Moreover, debt repayment often comes with stringent conditions imposed by creditors, such as austerity measures and structural reforms, which further undermine economic sovereignty and exacerbate social inequalities.

Examples abound of how paper money has been used as a tool of post-colonial control in various contexts. For instance, in Zimbabwe, hyperinflation driven by mismanagement of the currency and excessive money printing led to economic collapse and widespread social upheaval in the early 2000s. The Zimbabwean government, under President Robert Mugabe, resorted to printing money to finance unsustainable government spending, leading to hyperinflation rates that reached astronomical levels. Prices skyrocketed, the value of the Zimbabwean dollar plummeted, and the economy spiraled into chaos. Basic necessities became unaffordable for the average citizen, unemployment soared, and social services collapsed. The hyperinflation crisis in Zimbabwe serves as a stark reminder of the devastating consequences of unchecked money printing and economic mismanagement.

Similarly, in Argentina, currency devaluation and debt default during the 2001 economic crisis resulted in severe social unrest and political instability. Argentina, once hailed as an economic success story in the 1990s for its adherence to a fixed exchange rate regime pegged to the US dollar, experienced a dramatic reversal of fortune when the government defaulted on its external debt and abandoned the currency peg. The devaluation of the Argentine peso led to widespread impoverishment, as savings evaporated overnight and businesses collapsed. Riots broke out across the country, and successive governments struggled to restore stability and confidence in the economy. The Argentine economic crisis of 2001 serves as a cautionary tale of the dangers of unsustainable currency regimes and the perils of excessive debt accumulation.

In the upcoming chapter, we will delve into the transformative potential of the "peopleize" approach, which prioritizes people over profit, to revolutionize the existing money system and liberate individuals worldwide from the constraints imposed by artificially created mechanisms. The essence of the peopleize approach lies in its fundamental principle of placing the well-being and empowerment of individuals and communities at the forefront of economic decision-making, rather than prioritizing the accumulation of wealth and power by a privileged few.

By adopting a peopleize approach, societies can fundamentally reshape the dynamics of the money system to serve the interests of the broader populace, rather than perpetuating systems of exploitation and inequality. This paradigm shift involves reorienting the objectives of monetary policy and financial institutions towards promoting social justice, equitable wealth distribution, and sustainable development. Rather than allowing money to be wielded as a tool of control and domination by entrenched interests, the peopleize approach advocates for democratizing access to financial resources and empowering individuals to actively participate in shaping economic outcomes.

One of the key pillars of the peopleize approach is the recognition of money as a social construct that should serve the common good, rather than as a means of enriching a select few. By challenging the prevailing notion of money as a scarce commodity to be hoarded and controlled, societies can unlock its transformative potential as a tool for fostering economic justice and collective prosperity. This entails reimagining monetary systems based on principles of solidarity, cooperation, and mutual aid, rather than competition and exploitation.

Moreover, the peopleize approach emphasizes the importance of community-driven initiatives and grassroots movements in effecting meaningful change within the money system. By fostering participatory decision-making processes and decentralized forms of economic organization, communities can reclaim agency over their financial destinies and challenge the dominance of corporate interests and financial elites. This bottom-up approach to economic empowerment empowers individuals to become active agents of change in shaping the future of the money system.

In the chapters ahead, we will explore concrete strategies and examples of how the peopleize approach can be implemented to transform the money system and create a more just and equitable world for all. From community banking initiatives and alternative currencies to participatory budgeting and wealth redistribution policies, the peopleize approach offers a blueprint for building a more inclusive and democratic economy that prioritizes the needs and aspirations of ordinary people over the pursuit of profit and power. Through collective action and solidarity, we can harness the transformative potential of the peopleize approach to build a future where everyone has the opportunity to thrive and flourish.

Chapter ii

Rethinking Money for a Sustainable World

In this chapter, we embark on a journey to explore innovative approaches to currency design and financial systems that prioritize equity, sustainability, and community empowerment. By embracing the principles of the peopleize approach, we can reimagine the very foundations of our monetary systems to serve the common good rather than perpetuating systems of exploitation and inequality.

Interest-Free Finance:

Interest-Free Finance initiatives represent a beacon of hope for business owners and individuals seeking to break free from cycles of poverty and exploitation. These innovative models prioritize financial inclusion, social justice, and economic empowerment, offering a lifeline to individuals and communities who have been traditionally excluded from formal banking systems. By providing access to capital without the burden of interest, interest-free finance initiatives enable people to pursue entrepreneurial endeavors, invest in education and training, and improve their standard of living without the fear of falling into debt traps.

One notable example of interest-free microfinance is the **Grameen Bank** in Bangladesh, founded by Nobel laureate Muhammad Yunus. The Grameen Bank pioneered the concept of microcredit, providing small loans to business owners and individuals, particularly women, to start their own businesses and lift themselves out of poverty. Unlike traditional banks, the Grameen Bank does not charge interest on its loans, but rather operates on the principle of mutual trust and social responsibility. This interest-free model has empowered millions of people in Bangladesh and beyond to become entrepreneurs, generate sustainable income, and improve their quality of life.

The Islamic finance industry offers another example of interest-free microfinance through the concept of Islamic microfinance institutions (MFIs) such as Akhuwat in Pakistan. These institutions operate in accordance with Islamic principles, which prohibit the charging or paying of interest (riba). Instead, they provide qard al-hasan (benevolent loans) and other Sharia-compliant financial products to low-income individuals and communities. By leveraging the principles of profit-and-loss sharing, risk-sharing, and ethical investment, Islamic MFIs enable people to access capital for income-generating activities, education, and healthcare, thereby promoting social and economic development within their communities.

In addition to these examples, there are numerous grassroots organizations and community-based initiatives around the world that have embraced the concept of interest-free microfinance to empower marginalized populations. For instance, organizations like BRAC in Bangladesh, Women's World Banking in various countries, and Kiva, a global online crowdfunding platform, have all played significant roles in expanding access to interest-free microfinance and promoting economic empowerment at the grassroots level. These initiatives demonstrate the transformative potential of interest-free microfinance in uplifting communities, fostering entrepreneurship, and building resilient economies from the ground up.

Interest-free microfinance initiatives offer a powerful antidote to the predatory practices of traditional banking systems, providing business owners and individuals with the tools and resources they need to achieve economic self-sufficiency and social mobility. By prioritizing financial inclusion, ethical lending practices, and sustainable development, interest-free microfinance initiatives are paving the way for a more equitable and just financial system that empowers people to thrive.

Public Banking:

Public banking systems represent a paradigm shift in the financial landscape, prioritizing community development and economic resilience over profit maximization. Unlike their private counterparts, public banks are owned and operated by government entities or local authorities, with a mandate to serve the public interest and promote the well-being of communities. By harnessing public resources and leveraging local deposits, public banks are uniquely positioned to channel financial resources towards productive investments that benefit society as a whole, rather than enriching distant shareholders.

One significant benefit of public banking systems is their focus on community development and reinvestment in local economies. Unlike private banks that often prioritize shareholder returns and executive bonuses, public banks are guided by a broader set of social and economic objectives, including job creation, infrastructure development, and affordable housing. For example, the Bank of North Dakota, the only state-owned bank in the United States, has played a pivotal role in supporting local businesses, farmers, and homeowners through targeted lending programs and financial assistance initiatives. By directing capital towards productive investments within the state, the Bank of North Dakota has helped to spur economic growth, foster entrepreneurship, and mitigate the impact of economic downturns on local communities.

Similarly, public banking initiatives in countries like Germany, Switzerland, and India have demonstrated the potential for public banks to serve as engines of economic development and stability. In Germany, public savings banks (Sparkassen) and cooperative banks (Volksbanken) play a vital role in providing access to credit for small and medium-sized enterprises (SMEs), which are the backbone of the German economy. These institutions prioritize local lending and reinvest profits back into the communities they serve, contributing to regional prosperity and resilience.

Moreover, public banking systems have shown resilience during times of economic crisis, serving as stabilizing forces in turbulent financial environments. During the global financial crisis of 2008, for instance, public banks in countries like Germany and Brazil continued to provide credit to businesses and households, helping to mitigate the impact of the crisis on their respective economies. By maintaining liquidity and supporting critical sectors of the economy, public banks have proven to be effective counterbalances to the volatility and speculation that often characterize private financial markets.

Public banking systems offer a viable alternative to traditional private banking models, prioritizing community development, economic stability, and social equity. By harnessing public resources and aligning financial activities with the needs and priorities of local communities, public banks can play a transformative role in building more resilient, inclusive, and sustainable economies.

As the global financial landscape continues to evolve, public banking initiatives hold promise as powerful tools for promoting shared prosperity and advancing the public good.

Community Investment Funds:

Community Investment Funds represent a grassroots approach to economic development, empowering local communities to take control of their financial destinies and invest in projects that benefit the collective well-being. These funds operate on the principle of pooling resources from local stakeholders, including individuals, businesses, nonprofits, and local governments, to provide accessible and affordable financing for community-driven initiatives. Here is how they work:

Pooling Local Resources: Community Investment Funds gather financial contributions from various stakeholders within a community. This can include individual residents who invest their savings, local businesses looking to reinvest in the community, nonprofit organizations with a mission to support local causes, and even local government entities seeking to stimulate economic growth.

Low-Interest Loans for Community Projects: Once the funds are pooled, they are made available as low-interest loans for a wide range of community-driven projects. These projects can span various sectors, such as affordable housing developments, renewable energy installations, small business startups, community centers, educational programs, infrastructure improvements, and more.

Empowering Local Initiatives: Community Investment Funds empower local entrepreneurs, community groups, and organizations to access the capital they need to bring their ideas to life. This support is especially crucial for individuals and groups who may have difficulty securing financing through traditional banking channels due to lack of collateral or credit history.

Fostering Economic Self-Reliance: By providing an alternative source of funding outside of traditional banking institutions, Community Investment Funds foster economic self-reliance within communities. This reduces dependency on external financial institutions and empowers communities to chart their own economic course based on their unique needs and priorities.

Building Resilience: One of the key benefits of Community Investment Funds is their role in building resilience within communities. When local residents and businesses invest in projects that directly benefit their neighborhoods, they are more likely to see the long-term value and sustainability of these initiatives. This can lead to stronger social cohesion, economic stability, and a sense of pride in community accomplishments.

Examples of Community Investment Funds:

Local Development Funds: Many cities and towns have established local development funds that pool resources from residents, businesses, and local government to invest in projects that enhance the quality of life in the community. For example, a local development fund might provide funding for the renovation of a historic downtown area, the creation of a community garden, or the establishment of a small business incubator.

Community Land Trusts: Community land trusts are nonprofit organizations that acquire and hold land for the benefit of the community. They often rely on funding from Community Investment Funds to purchase land and develop affordable housing, community gardens, and recreational spaces. Residents have a stake in the trust and participate in decision-making processes.

Microfinance Programs: In some communities, Community Investment Funds are used to support microfinance programs that provide small loans to aspiring entrepreneurs, particularly those from marginalized or underserved communities. These loans help individuals start businesses, create jobs, and stimulate local economic growth.

Green Revolving Funds: Environmental initiatives also benefit from Community Investment Funds. Green revolving funds, for instance, are used by universities, municipalities, and businesses to invest in energy efficiency upgrades, renewable energy projects, and sustainable infrastructure. The cost savings from these projects are then reinvested into the fund for future sustainability initiatives.

Community Investment Funds represent a powerful tool for empowering communities, fostering economic self-reliance, and building resilience. By harnessing the collective resources and expertise of local stakeholders, these funds enable communities to invest in projects that align with their values, priorities, and vision for a sustainable and thriving future. Through collaboration, inclusivity, and shared ownership, Community Investment Funds pave the way for vibrant, resilient, and prosperous communities.

Resource-Based Economies:

Resource-Based Economies represent a shift towards prioritizing the sustainable management and equitable distribution of a country's natural resources. Instead of solely focusing on the extraction and export of raw materials, these economies aim to harness their natural wealth in a way that benefits the entire population, protects the environment, and ensures long-term economic stability. Here is an in-depth look at how these economies work and examples of countries transitioning towards this model:

Sustainable Resource Management: Resource-Based Economies emphasize the sustainable use of natural resources to avoid depletion and environmental degradation. This involves implementing policies and practices that balance economic development with environmental conservation. Countries prioritize technologies and methods that minimize the environmental footprint of resource extraction, such as responsible mining practices, reforestation programs, and renewable energy development.

Diversification of Revenue Streams: Instead of relying solely on the export of raw materials, Resource-Based Economies seek to diversify their revenue streams by adding value to their natural resources. This includes investing in downstream industries such as processing, manufacturing, and technology development. By adding value to raw materials before export, countries can capture a larger share of the economic benefits and create more job opportunities for their citizens.

Equitable Distribution of Wealth: A key principle of Resource-Based Economies is to ensure that the wealth generated from natural resources is distributed equitably among the population. This involves implementing fair tax policies, revenue-sharing mechanisms with local communities, and social programs that benefit all citizens. The goal is to reduce income inequality and improve the overall quality of life for everyone, especially those living in resource-rich regions.

Examples of Resource-Based Economies:

Norway: Norway is often cited as a prime example of a country with a successful resource-based economy. The discovery of oil in the North Sea in the 1960s transformed Norway's economy, but the government took a strategic approach to managing this newfound wealth. The country established the Government Pension Fund Global, also known as the "Norwegian Oil Fund," to save and invest a portion of its oil revenue for future generations. Norway also implemented strict environmental regulations for oil extraction and invested heavily in renewable energy sources such as hydropower.

Chile: Chile is another example of a country that has transitioned towards a resource-based economy, particularly in the mining sector. The country is one of the world's largest producers of copper, and it has implemented policies to ensure that mining activities benefit the entire population. Chile established a sovereign wealth fund, the Economic and Social Stabilization Fund, to save a portion of its mining revenue for times of economic uncertainty. The government also provides social programs and infrastructure development in mining communities to improve living standards.

Botswana: Botswana is known for its successful management of diamond resources. The country established the Debswana Diamond Company, a joint venture between the government and diamond mining company De Beers, to oversee diamond mining operations. Botswana has used its diamond revenue to invest in education, healthcare, and infrastructure, leading to significant improvements in human development indicators.

Costa Rica: While not traditionally seen as a resource-based economy, Costa Rica has made strides in sustainable resource management, particularly in its focus on eco-tourism and renewable energy. The country has preserved a significant portion of its land as national parks and protected areas, capitalizing on its natural beauty to attract tourists. Costa Rica also generates a substantial portion of its electricity from renewable sources such as hydroelectric, wind, and geothermal power.

Lessons Learned and Challenges: Transitioning towards a resource-based economy comes with its own set of challenges and considerations. Governments must strike a delicate balance between promoting economic development and protecting the environment. Additionally, there is a need for strong governance, transparency, and accountability to ensure that the benefits of resource wealth reach all segments of society. Furthermore, diversification of the economy is crucial to reduce vulnerability to fluctuations in commodity prices and global demand.

Resource-Based Economies offer a pathway towards sustainable development, equitable wealth distribution, and environmental stewardship. By managing natural resources responsibly, diversifying revenue streams, and ensuring that the benefits reach all citizens, countries can create a foundation for long-term prosperity and well-being. The examples of Norway, Chile, Botswana, and Costa Rica demonstrate the potential of this model when implemented with strategic planning, strong governance, and a commitment to sustainability.

Participatory Budgeting:

Participatory Budgeting (PB) is a democratic process that empowers community members to directly participate in decisions about the allocation of public funds. Through PB initiatives, residents have the opportunity to identify, discuss, and prioritize local needs, ultimately influencing how public budgets are spent. This grassroots approach to budgeting aims to foster transparency, accountability, and civic engagement within communities. Here's an in-depth look at how PB works and examples of successful implementations:

Direct Community Involvement: Participatory Budgeting allows residents to play an active role in the decision-making process regarding public spending. Community members come together in assemblies, meetings, or online platforms to brainstorm ideas, propose projects, and discuss priorities for their neighborhood or municipality.

Proposal Development: During PB processes, residents can submit project proposals that address various community needs, such as infrastructure improvements, park renovations, public transportation enhancements, cultural programs, and social services. These proposals are then reviewed, refined, and developed into feasible projects with the help of technical experts.

Voting and Project Selection: Once a list of proposals is finalized, residents are given the opportunity to vote on which projects should receive funding. This voting process is typically open to all community members, including adults, youth, and sometimes even non-citizens. Projects with the highest number of votes are prioritized for implementation.

Budget Allocation: Participatory Budgeting often involves a portion of the public budget being set aside specifically for community-chosen projects. This dedicated fund allows residents to directly influence how public resources are allocated, ensuring that local needs and priorities are addressed.

Examples of Participatory Budgeting:

Porto Alegre, Brazil: Porto Alegre is widely recognized as a pioneer in Participatory Budgeting, having implemented the process since the late 1980s. In this Brazilian city, residents have the opportunity to directly decide on approximately 20% of the municipal budget. Through assemblies and neighborhood meetings, residents discuss and vote on projects ranging from sanitation improvements to healthcare facilities and community centers.

New York City, USA: New York City launched Participatory Budgeting in several of its districts, allowing residents to decide how to allocate part of the city's capital budget. In these districts, residents propose and vote on projects such as park renovations, street lighting upgrades, school improvements, and public art installations.

Paris, France: The city of Paris introduced Participatory Budgeting in 2014, engaging residents in decisions about the allocation of €500 million over six years. Parisians can suggest and vote on projects related to green spaces, sustainable transportation, cultural events, and social services. The process has led to the creation of new bike lanes, community gardens, and public Wi-Fi hotspots.

La Paz, Bolivia: La Paz implemented Participatory Budgeting to empower citizens, particularly marginalized groups, in decision-making processes. Residents of this Bolivian city have influenced projects such as the construction of schools, health clinics, sports facilities, and public spaces. The process has helped bridge gaps in social inclusion and improve the quality of life for many residents.

Socially Responsible Investing:

Socially Responsible Investing (SRI) involves investment strategies that consider both financial returns and positive social or environmental impact. Instead of solely focusing on maximizing profits, SRI seeks to align investment decisions with ethical, social, and environmental values. Here's a closer look at how SRI works and examples of its implementation:

Investment Screening: SRI involves screening potential investments based on criteria related to environmental, social, and governance (ESG) factors. Companies are evaluated on their sustainability practices, labor standards, treatment of employees, community engagement, diversity policies, and environmental impact. Investments are then made in companies that meet these responsible criteria.

Positive Impact Investing: SRI also includes actively seeking out investments that have a positive impact on society and the environment. This can involve investing in renewable energy projects, sustainable agriculture initiatives, affordable housing developments, clean technology companies, and social enterprises that address pressing social issues.

Shareholder Advocacy: SRI investors often engage in shareholder advocacy to encourage companies to improve their ESG practices. Shareholders may file resolutions, attend annual meetings, and engage in dialogues with company management to advocate for changes such as reducing carbon emissions, increasing diversity on boards, or improving labor standards.

Examples of Socially Responsible Investing:

Renewable Energy: SRI funds often invest in renewable energy companies that produce solar, wind, and hydroelectric power. These investments contribute to the transition towards a low-carbon economy and reduce reliance on fossil fuels.

Impact Bonds: SRI funds may invest in impact bonds issued by organizations working on social issues such as education, healthcare, poverty alleviation, and affordable housing. These bonds provide financial support to projects that generate measurable social or environmental benefits.

Ethical Consumer Goods: SRI funds may invest in companies that produce ethical consumer goods, such as fair trade products, organic foods, eco-friendly clothing, and sustainable household products. These investments support businesses that prioritize environmental sustainability and ethical labor practices.

Community Development: SRI funds may allocate capital to community development financial institutions (CDFIs) that provide loans and financial services to underserved communities. These investments support initiatives such as affordable housing, small business development, and job creation in disadvantaged areas.

Participatory Budgeting and Socially Responsible Investing are powerful tools for promoting democracy, sustainability, and social equity. Through PB, communities can directly shape the allocation of public funds, ensuring that resources are directed towards projects that benefit the common good. SRI, on the other hand, allows investors to align their financial goals with their values, supporting companies and initiatives that contribute to a more sustainable and socially conscious world. Together, these approaches empower individuals, communities, and investors to make positive impacts and create a brighter future for all.

Indeed, while these programs such as Participatory Budgeting and Socially

Responsible Investing represent significant steps towards more equitable and sustainable societies, they are still operating within the framework of the existing colonial money system. This system, rooted in historical legacies of exploitation and unequal power dynamics, can limit the effectiveness of these initiatives due to external factors that influence currency value and financial mechanisms.

The colonial money system, inherited from a history of colonization and imperialism, is deeply entrenched in global economic structures. It perpetuates inequalities through mechanisms such as currency manipulation, debt dependencies, and unequal trade relationships. As a result, even well-intentioned programs can face challenges in achieving their full potential when operating within this framework.

In the upcoming chapter, we will delve into the concept of each country creating its own new paper money system. This radical idea seeks to break away from the constraints of the colonial money system and empower nations to take control of their monetary policies, currency valuation, and economic destinies. Here's an overview of what we will explore:

▷ **Sovereign Monetary Policies**: Each country creating its own paper money system would mean reclaiming sovereignty over monetary policies. This includes the ability to set interest rates, control inflation, and regulate the supply of money in circulation based on the country's specific economic needs and goals.

- **Currency Valuation**: Instead of being subject to the fluctuations of global currency markets, countries value of their currency will be equal.

- **Elimination of Debt Dependencies**: Creating a new paper money system would also allow countries to break free from debt dependencies on international financial institutions. By issuing their own currency for public spending and investment, nations can reduce reliance on borrowing from external sources, thereby avoiding the burdens of interest payments and structural adjustment programs.

- **Fostering Economic Independence**: A new paper money system empowers countries to pursue economic policies that prioritize the well-being of their citizens and the sustainable development of their economies. This includes investing in infrastructure, social programs, education, healthcare, and sustainable technologies without external interference.

- **Promoting Fair Trade and Economic Justice**: With control over their currency, countries can establish fair trade practices that benefit local industries and workers. They can implement trade agreements that protect domestic markets while fostering equitable economic relationships with other nations.

By examining the possibilities of each country creating its own new paper money system, we open the door to envisioning a more just, equitable, and sustainable global economic order. This radical departure from the colonial money system offers the promise of economic independence, self-determination, and the ability to shape financial policies in alignment with the needs and values of each nation and its people. In the following chapter, we will delve deeper into the practicalities, implications, and potential pathways towards realizing this transformative vision.

Chapter iii

PEOPLEIZE Currency for Equity and Sustainability:
Redefining the Logic and Value of Money

Redefining the Logic and Value of Money requires us to challenge deeply ingrained perceptions and assumptions about the nature of currency. Often viewed as an inherent measure of worth, money is traditionally associated with tangible assets or commodities, such as gold or silver. However, delving deeper into the essence of money reveals its fundamentally artificial nature, a construct whose value is derived not from any intrinsic worth but from collective human agreement and societal structures.

At its core, money is a social and symbolic construct, a medium of exchange that facilitates transactions and enables economic activity within societies. Its value is not inherent in the physical form of paper bills or metal coins but is instead imbued by the trust and confidence that individuals and institutions place in it. This trust is rooted in the belief that others will also accept this form of currency in exchange for goods, services, or other forms of value. In essence, money is a shared illusion, a collective agreement that grants it the power to represent and facilitate the exchange of goods and services within an economy.

Highlighting the artificial nature of money invites us to reconsider its value not as an absolute measure of worth but as a dynamic and evolving concept shaped by human interactions and societal norms. The value of money fluctuates not only based on economic factors such as inflation or interest rates but also on broader social, cultural, and political dynamics. For example, the value of a currency may be influenced by perceptions of stability, trust in government institutions, or even cultural beliefs about the role of money in society.

By emphasizing that the value of money is derived from human agreement, we challenge the notion that wealth and worth are synonymous. The accumulation of money does not inherently equate to value or moral worth; rather, it reflects the ability to navigate and succeed within existing economic systems. This reframing encourages us to consider alternative measures of value beyond monetary wealth, such as social capital, community well-being, and environmental sustainability.

Moreover, recognizing the artificial nature of money opens up possibilities for reimagining and redesigning our monetary systems to better serve the needs of society. It invites us to question the structures and mechanisms that perpetuate inequality and financial exclusion, such as interest rates, debt-based economies, and wealth concentration. By understanding that money is a human creation, we empower ourselves to shape its value and purpose in ways that align with our collective values and aspirations.

In redefining the value of money challenges us to transcend its material form and see it as a social construct shaped by human agreement. By acknowledging its artificial nature, we open the door to new possibilities for designing more equitable, inclusive, and sustainable economic systems. This shift in perspective invites us to consider the true purpose of money, to facilitate exchange, promote well-being, and serve the common good of all members of society.

PEOPLEIZE Currency Alternatives:

PEOPLEIZE Currency Alternatives represent a revolutionary approach to monetary systems, aiming to challenge the dominance of centralized banking institutions and promote financial inclusivity and autonomy. In exploring the potential of decentralized currencies, we embark on a journey to reimagine the very nature of money itself, envisioning a world where financial transactions are conducted peer-to-peer, without the need for intermediaries or centralized authorities. While cryptocurrencies like Bitcoin have garnered significant attention in this space, we will explore the concept of a state-owned paper money as a tangible alternative that harnesses the principles of decentralization and decolonization.

Imagine a state-owned paper money system, issued and regulated by governments and local authorities, but operating independently of traditional banking institutions. This alternative currency would be decentralized in nature, meaning that transactions would be recorded on a distributed ledger maintained by a network of participants, rather than being controlled by a single entity. By leveraging blockchain technology or similar decentralized protocols, this PEOPLEIZE currency system would ensure transparency, security, and trust in financial transactions, while empowering individuals to transact directly with one another.

One of the key benefits of a PEOPLEIZE state-owned paper money system is its potential to democratize access to capital and financial services. Unlike traditional banking systems that often exclude marginalized communities and small businesses from accessing credit and financial resources, this alternative currency system would be inclusive and accessible to all. Individuals and businesses would have the opportunity to participate in the issuance and distribution of the currency, enabling greater financial empowerment and economic resilience at the grassroots level.

Moreover, a state-owned paper money system could serve as a catalyst for economic development and innovation. It have no interest rates or making money off of loans. By providing a stable and reliable medium of exchange, this alternative currency would facilitate trade and commerce, spur investment in local economies, and stimulate entrepreneurial activity. Additionally, the decentralized nature of the currency would foster innovation in financial services, opening up new avenues for peer-to-peer lending, crowdfunding, and other forms of decentralized finance (DeFi) that empower individuals to take control of their financial futures.

Furthermore, a state-owned paper money system would promote financial sovereignty and independence from external influences. Unlike conventional currencies that are subject to manipulation by central banks and financial institutions, this alternative currency would be immune to inflationary pressures and currency devaluation, ensuring the preservation of wealth and purchasing power for individuals and communities. By breaking free from the constraints of centralized banking systems, individuals would have greater control over their financial destinies, fostering a more equitable and resilient economy for all.

In exploring the potential of decentralized currencies through the lens of a PEOPLEIZE state-owned paper money system offers a glimpse into a future where financial systems are democratized, inclusive, and resilient. By harnessing the principles of decentralization and democratization, this alternative currency system has the potential to revolutionize the way we think about money, empower individuals and communities, and build a more equitable and sustainable economy for future generations.

How would it work:

The implementation of the PEOPLEIZE paper money system envisions a transformative shift in the way currency operates within economies, emphasizing principles of equality, sustainability, and collective well-being. Here is how it would work:

▷ **National Currency Creation**: Each country would have the authority to print its own PEOPLEIZE paper money, a form of currency designed for everyday transactions within the country. This national currency would serve as a medium of exchange, unit of account, and store of value, functioning much like traditional fiat currencies. However, the key difference lies in its principles and mechanisms of operation.

▷ **Equal Value Across Nations**: The value of each country's PEOPLEIZE paper money would be standardized and equalized across all participating nations. This means that one unit of PEOPLEIZE in one country would have the same value as one unit of PEOPLEIZE in another country. This equality in value eliminates disparities caused by fluctuating exchange rates, making international trade and collaboration simpler and more efficient.

- **Elimination of Artificial Controls**: Crucially, the PEOPLEIZE paper money system would be free from artificial mechanisms that manipulate or control the value of the currency. This includes the absence of interest rates, inflationary pressures, or other forms of monetary policy interventions that traditionally influence currency values.

- **Facilitating Everyday Transactions**: PEOPLEIZE paper money would be used by individuals, businesses, and organizations for everyday transactions, such as buying goods and services, paying bills, and conducting local and national trade. Its ease of use and stability in value would make it a reliable and efficient medium of exchange, fostering economic activity and financial stability within each country.

- **International Trade and Collaboration**: Beyond domestic use, PEOPLEIZE paper money would facilitate international trade and collaboration among nations. Countries could engage in trade agreements and partnerships knowing that the value of their currency remains consistent and equitable with that of their trading partners. This would streamline cross-border transactions and promote economic cooperation on a global scale.

▷ **Shift in Focus**: Importantly, the PEOPLEIZE paper money system aims to shift the focus of individuals and societies from the pursuit of accumulating more money to the collective goal of living together in harmony and creating a sustainable Earth for all. This reframing of values encourages people to prioritize shared well-being, social harmony, and environmental stewardship over material wealth and individual accumulation.

▷ **Promoting Sustainable Practices**: The PEOPLEIZE paper money system would incentivize sustainable practices and responsible consumption patterns. By valuing collaboration, community support, and environmental conservation, the system encourages individuals and businesses to make choices that contribute to the long-term health and sustainability of the planet.

▷ **Empowering Communities**: Communities would have greater control and autonomy over their economic activities, as the PEOPLEIZE paper money system empowers local businesses, cooperatives, and initiatives. This localization of economic transactions fosters resilience, diversity, and inclusivity within communities, reducing dependency on external forces and promoting self-reliance.

In essence, the PEOPLEIZE paper money system represents a bold vision for a new economic paradigm, one that prioritizes equality, sustainability, and the collective well-being of humanity. By reimagining the purpose and function of money, this system aims to create a world where financial systems serve the needs of people and the planet, fostering a harmonious and prosperous future for all.

People Ownership of PEOPLEIZE Public Funds:

People Ownership of PEOPLEIZE Public Funds embodies the fundamental principle that taxpayers, as contributors to public finances, are the rightful owners of these resources. This principle emphasizes the notion that public funds are not the domain of governments or institutions alone, but rather belong to the collective populace whose contributions sustain the functioning of the state. Central to this concept are ideals of transparency, accountability, and citizen participation in the management and allocation of public resources, with the overarching goal of advancing the common good and fostering a more equitable and inclusive society.

At its core, People Ownership of PEOPLEIZE Public Funds challenges the traditional top-down approach to public finance, where decisions on budgeting, spending, and investment are often made behind closed doors by government officials and financial institutions. Instead, it advocates for a democratic and participatory process where taxpayers have a direct say in how their contributions are utilized for the benefit of society as a whole.

Transparency plays a pivotal role in this paradigm, ensuring that citizens have access to information about government expenditures, revenues, and financial transactions. By making this information readily available and easily understandable, taxpayers can hold their governments accountable for how public funds are managed and allocated. This transparency not only builds trust between citizens and the government but also enables informed decision-making and oversight of public finances.

People Ownership of PEOPLEIZE Public Funds calls for mechanisms of citizen participation in the budgeting process, such as participatory budgeting initiatives. These programs empower citizens to directly influence budget priorities, allocate resources to community projects, and monitor the implementation of public programs.

Example of People Ownership of PEOPLEIZE Public Funds in Action:

Let's imagine a hypothetical scenario where a country, let's call it "Equitopia," adopts the People Ownership of PEOPLEIZE Public Funds system. Equitopia is a diverse nation with a range of economic activities, from urban centers to rural communities, all contributing to the national economy.

1. Transparent Financial Data:

The government of Equitopia begins by implementing a robust system of transparency. All financial data related to public funds, including expenditures, revenues, and investments, are made easily accessible to the public. Equitopians can log into a user-friendly online platform where they can view real-time updates on how their tax contributions are being used.

2. Participatory Budgeting:

Equitopia launches a participatory budgeting initiative where citizens can actively participate in the allocation of public funds. Here's how it works:

- **Proposal Phase:** Any Equitopian citizen or community group can submit proposals for projects they believe will benefit society. These proposals could range from building new community centers to investing in renewable energy projects.

- **Review and Discussion:** A dedicated online forum allows citizens to discuss and provide feedback on each proposal. Experts and government officials are also present to answer questions and provide technical insights.

- **Voting:** After the review period, citizens are given the opportunity to vote on which projects should receive funding. They can do this through the same online platform, ensuring accessibility for all.

- **Allocation:** Based on the results of the voting, the government allocates the PEOPLEIZE public funds to the selected projects. The allocation process is transparent and publicly documented, allowing citizens to track the progress of each initiative.

3. Community Empowerment:

In a rural area of Equitopia, a farming cooperative proposes a project to improve irrigation systems and access to markets for small-scale farmers. Equitopians in the region rally behind the initiative, seeing it as a way to boost local economies and support sustainable agriculture.

- **Proposal Submission:** The cooperative submits a detailed proposal outlining the benefits of the project, estimated costs, and expected outcomes.

- **Public Discussion:** Equitopians from neighboring villages engage in online discussions, sharing stories of how improved irrigation could increase crop yields and incomes for their families.

- **Voting Process:** During the voting phase, citizens from across Equitopia, not just the rural areas, show their support for the project. They recognize the interconnectedness of their nation's economy and the importance of uplifting all communities.

- **Funding Approval:** With overwhelming public support, the project receives a significant portion of the PEOPLEIZE public funds allocated for community development.

4. Impact and Results:

Months later, Equitopia celebrates the completion of the irrigation project. Small-scale farmers now have reliable access to water, reducing crop loss during dry seasons. This leads to increased yields, higher incomes, and a thriving local economy.

- **Empowered Communities:** The success of the project inspires other communities to propose and implement their own initiatives. Equitopians feel a sense of ownership over their public funds, knowing that their contributions directly impact the well-being of their fellow citizens.

- **Trust in Government:** Transparency and citizen participation have strengthened trust between the government and the people. Equitopians have witnessed firsthand the government's commitment to listening to their needs and acting in the best interest of society.

- **Equitable Development:** Across urban and rural areas alike, Equitopia experiences balanced and inclusive development. The PEOPLEIZE public funds system has ensured that no community is left behind, fostering a sense of unity and shared prosperity.

In this hypothetical example, People Ownership of PEOPLEIZE Public Funds transforms Equitopia into a model of democratic governance and equitable development. By embracing transparency, participatory decision-making, and community empowerment, the nation paves the way for a more inclusive and prosperous future for all its citizens.

Another key aspect of this concept is accountability, holding government officials and institutions responsible for their stewardship of public funds. Through mechanisms such as audits, public hearings, and independent oversight bodies, taxpayers can ensure that funds are used efficiently, effectively, and in accordance with the needs and interests of the populace.

Furthermore, People Ownership of Public Funds envisions a shift in the purpose of money itself, viewing it not as an end in itself but as a tool for documenting daily transactions and facilitating economic activities. In this vision, the amount of money printed by a country becomes less significant than its role in enabling individuals to pursue their aspirations, create opportunities for all members of society, and contribute to the greater good.

People Ownership of Public Funds represents a paradigm shift towards a more democratic, transparent, and participatory approach to public finance. By recognizing taxpayers as the rightful owners of public resources and advocating for their active engagement in decision-making, this concept aims to build trust, promote accountability, and foster a sense of collective responsibility for the equitable and sustainable use of public funds. Ultimately, it envisions a society where the purpose of money transcends mere economic transactions, becoming a tool for advancing the well-being and aspirations of all members of the community.

The PEOPLEIZE Currency for Equity and Sustainability presents a transformative vision of the future of finance. By challenging the dominance of centralized banking institutions and advocating for financial inclusivity, autonomy, and transparency, this revolutionary approach aims to reshape the very essence of money. Through a state-owned PEOPLEIZE paper money system, decentralized in nature and immune to the manipulations of traditional currencies, PEOPLEIZE offers a pathway to democratized, inclusive, and resilient financial systems. It envisions a world where individuals and communities have greater control over their financial destinies, fostering economic empowerment at the grassroots level. With a focus on equality, sustainability, and collective well-being, PEOPLEIZE paves the way for a more harmonious and prosperous global economy, where the purpose of money transcends mere accumulation and serves the greater good of people and the planet. Join us on this journey of redefining the logic and value of money, and together, let's create a future where finance works for everyone, everywhere.

MY HEARTFELT GRATITUDE

In composing the words for "PEOPLEIZE - Decolonizing Money for Global Equality - Utilizing Currency for Equity, Not Colonialism," I find myself immersed in a profound sense of gratitude. This endeavor, delving into collaborative governance, community harmony, sustainability, and the pursuit of shared prosperity, has been a transformative odyssey. To every reader who has joined me on this journey, I extend my heartfelt thanks.

To those who have dared to challenge conventional norms, to dream expansively, and to envision a world defined by unity and justice, your unwavering dedication to this transformative vision has been the driving force behind "PEOPLEIZE: Decolonizing Governmental System." I am deeply grateful for your courage and steadfast commitment to pushing the boundaries of what is possible.

Producing a work of such magnitude is never a solitary effort. I am immensely thankful to the countless individuals who have contributed, each in their own way, to the realization of "PEOPLEIZE - Decolonizing Money for Global Equality - Utilizing Currency for Equity, Not Colonialism." Your insights, support, and shared passion have been instrumental in bringing this vision to life.

To the pioneers who advocate for the transformative power of collaboration, to those who champion equality, justice, and empathy, and to every advocate for a more just world, this book stands as a testament to our collective aspirations. May the ideas conveyed within its pages ignite dialogue, inspire action, and catalyze positive change in our communities and beyond.

To all who steadfastly believe in a future where peace, equality, harmony, and prosperity are shared by all, I offer my deepest gratitude. "PEOPLEIZE - Decolonizing Money for Global Equality - Utilizing Currency for Equity, Not Colonialism" transcends mere literature; it serves as a beacon guiding us towards a brighter tomorrow. Thank you for accompanying me on this extraordinary journey.

With heartfelt gratitude and warm wishes,
xoxo Einar